a · Dragon · in · a · Wagon

Lynley Dodd

Gareth Stevens Publishing
A WORLD ALMANAC EDUCATION GROUP COMPANY

Susie Fogg
took Sam her dog
along by Jackson's Stream.
And as they walked
Susie talked,
and dreamed a wishful
dream.

"Sam," she said,
"You're very good,
you never bark or bite.
The holes you dig
are not TOO big,
and you're always home
at night.
But just for once
it might be fun
if you changed from dog," she said.
"To something HUGE
or something FIERCE
or something ODD
instead.

Let me see,
you could be...
a dragon
in a wagon,

a bat
with a hat,

a snake
eating cake,

a gnu
with the flu,

a whale
in a pail,

a chimp
with a limp,

a yak
on his back,

a moose
on the loose,

a lizard
in a blizzard

or a shark
in the dark."

A mossy log
tripped Susie Fogg,
she tumbled to the ground.
And as she wiped off
all the mud,
she looked behind
and found...

No sharks, no bats,
no hairy yaks,
no dragons in a jam.
Just the face,
the friendly face,
the DOGGY face
of Sam.

For a free color catalog describing Gareth Stevens' list of high-quality books and multimedia programs, call 1-800-542-2595 (USA) or 1-800-461-9120 (Canada). Gareth Stevens Publishing's Fax: (414) 225-0377.

Other GOLD STAR FIRST READER Millennium Editions:

and also by Lynley Dodd:

Hairy Maclary from Donaldson's Dairy
Hairy Maclary Scattercat
Hairy Maclary and Zachary Quack
Hairy Maclary's Caterwaul Caper
Hairy Maclary's Rumpus at the Vet
The Smallest Turtle
SNIFF-SNUFF-SNAP!

Hairy Maclary, Sit
Hairy Maclary's Showbusiness
The Minister's Cat ABC
Schnitzel von Krumm Forget-Me-Not
Slinky Malinki Catflaps

Library of Congress Cataloging-in-Publication Data

Dodd, Lynley.
    A dragon in a wagon / by Lynley Dodd.
       p. cm. — (Gold star first readers)
      Summary: For the sake of variety, Susie imagines that her friendly dog Sam is a series of more exotic creatures, from a dragon in a wagon to a shark in the dark.
      ISBN 0-8368-2687-6 (lib. bdg.)
      [1. Dogs—Fiction. 2. Imagination—Fiction. 3. Animals—Fiction. 4. Stories in rhyme.] I. Title. II. Series.
PZ8.3.D637Dr   2000
[E]—dc21   00-029156

This edition first published in 2000 by
Gareth Stevens Publishing
A World Almanac Education Group Company
1555 North RiverCenter Drive, Suite 201
Milwaukee, WI 53212 USA

First published in New Zealand by Mallinson Rendel Publishers Ltd. Original © 1988 by Lynley Dodd.

Printed in the United States of America

1 2 3 4 5 6 7 8 9 04 03 02 01 00

12672